Peter Rabbit's™ Little Treasury

Peter Rabbit's™ Little Treasury

FREDERICK WARNE

FREDERICK WARNE
Published by the Penguin Group
Penguin Books Ltd, 27 Wrights Lane, London W8 5TZ, England
Penguin Putnam Inc., 375 Hudson Street, New York, NY 10014, USA
Penguin Books Australia Ltd, Ringwood, Victoria, Australia
Penguin Books Canada Ltd, 10 Alcorn Avenue, Toronto, Ontario, Canada M4V 3B2
Penguin Books (N.Z.) Ltd, 182-190 Wairau Road, Auckland 10, New Zealand
Penguin Books (South Africa) (Pty) Ltd, 5 Watkins Street, Denver Ext 4, Johannesburg 2094, South Africa
Penguin Books India (P) Ltd, 11 Community Centre, Panchsheel Park, New Delhi - 110 017, India

Penguin Books Ltd, Registered Offices: Harmondsworth, Middlesex, England

First published 2000

ISBN 0 7232 4670 X

Printed and bound in Hong Kong by Imago Publishing Ltd

CONTENTS

A Background to the Tales

The Tale of Peter Rabbit

Beatrix Potter enjoyed writing letters to children, and a picture letter dated September 4th 1893 was the origin of *The Tale of Peter Rabbit*.

Although there is not one specific local setting for the story, the real Peter Rabbit, who was Beatrix's pet rabbit, is well known. She never forgot the hero of her first little book. In one of her privately printed copies of *The Tale of Peter Rabbit* she wrote, 'In affectionate remembrance of poor old Peter Rabbit ... whatever the limitations of his intellect or shortcomings of his fur, and his ears and toes, his disposition was uniformly amiable and his temper unfailingly sweet. An affectionate companion and a quiet friend.'

The Tale of Tom Kitten

By the time Beatrix Potter started writing *The Tale of Tom Kitten*, she had owned Hill Top Farm, in the Lake District village of Sawrey, for a year. Both house and garden feature in the story.

When Beatrix began sketching the cat family for *The Tale of Tom Kitten* she borrowed a kitten, which proved to be a mischievous model – rather like Tom Kitten himself. On July 18th 1906, she wrote, 'I have borrowed a kitten ... It is very young and pretty and a most fearful pickle.'

Beatrix Potter was rather fond of ducks and named several generations of ducks after the fictional Puddle-ducks. She was a great perfectionist and never felt comfortable with her drawings of cats and kittens, but she felt the duck drawings helped, and pronounced herself satisfied with her copy of the finished book, writing to her publisher, 'I am much pleased with "Tom Kitten"'.

The Tale of Squirrel Nutkin

The Tale of Squirrel Nutkin took shape in another of Beatrix Potter's picture letters, this time to Norah Moore, another of her ex-governess's children. The letter was illustrated by twelve pen-and-ink sketches, and Beatrix borrowed the letter back from Norah to use it as a basis for the book.

Beatrix had some trouble finding a model for Nutkin and his cousins. On January 17th 1903, she wrote to a friend, 'I have got a very pretty little model; I bought two but they weren't a pair, and fought so frightfully that I had to get rid of the handsomer – and most savage one – The other squirrel is rather a nice little animal, but half of one ear has been bitten off, which spoils his appearance!'

Beatrix was very pleased about the success of her squirrel book, although she reacted with typical modesty. 'I am delighted to hear such a good account of Nutkin, I never thought when I was drawing it that it would be such a success . . .'

The Tale of Johnny Town-Mouse

The Tale of Johnny Town-Mouse is set in Lake District surroundings: Johnny lives in the town of Hawkshead, while Timmy Willie has his home in a Sawrey garden. Old Diamond, Beatrix's farm horse, pulls the carrier's cart (her favourite of all the pictures), and the cook is a local woman, Mrs Rogerson. Johnny Town-mouse himself is based on a Doctor Parsons, who would bring his long bag of clubs to play golf with Beatrix's husband, William Heelis.

The theme of the tale is taken from a fable by Aesop, and Beatrix dedicated the story to 'Aesop in the shadows'. Her sight was failing, and she despaired of the drawings. 'I cannot see to put colour in them.' However the country pictures, in particular, are as delightful as ever.

The Tale of Peter Rabbit

Once upon a time there were four little Rabbits, and their names were—

Flopsy,
Mopsy,
Cotton-tail,
and Peter.

They lived with their Mother in a sand-bank, underneath the root of a very big fir-tree.

'NOW, my dears,' said old Mrs. Rabbit one morning, 'you may go into the fields or down the lane, but don't go into Mr. McGregor's garden: your Father had an accident there; he was put in a pie by Mrs. McGregor.'

'NOW run along, and don't get into mischief. I am going out.'

THEN old Mrs. Rabbit took a basket and her umbrella, and went through the wood to the baker's. She bought a loaf of brown bread and five currant buns.

FLOPSY, Mopsy, and Cottontail, who were good little bunnies, went down the lane to gather blackberries:

BUT Peter, who was very naughty, ran straight away to Mr. McGregor's garden, and squeezed under the gate!

FIRST he ate some lettuces and some French beans; and then he ate some radishes;

AND then, feeling rather sick, he went to look for some parsley.

BUT round the end of a cucumber frame, whom should he meet but Mr. McGregor!

Mr. McGREGOR was on his hands
and knees planting out young
cabbages, but he jumped up and ran
after Peter, waving a rake and calling
out, 'Stop thief!'

PETER was most dreadfully frightened; he rushed all over the garden,
for he had forgotten the way back to
the gate.

He lost one of his shoes among the
cabbages, and the other shoe amongst
the potatoes.

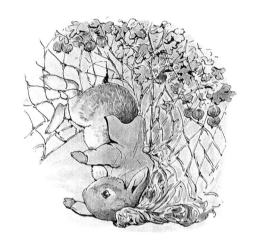

AFTER losing them, he ran on four legs and went faster, so that I think he might have got away altogether if he had not unfortunately run into a gooseberry net, and got caught by the large buttons on his jacket. It was a blue jacket with brass buttons, quite new.

PETER gave himself up for lost, and shed big tears; but his sobs were overheard by some friendly sparrows, who flew to him in great excitement, and implored him to exert himself.

MR. McGREGOR came up with a sieve, which he intended to pop upon the top of Peter; but Peter wriggled out just in time, leaving his jacket behind him.

A ND rushed into the tool-shed, and
jumped into a can. It would have
been a beautiful thing to hide in, if it
had not had so much water in it.

M R. McGREGOR was quite sure
that Peter was somewhere in the
tool-shed, perhaps hidden underneath a
flower-pot. He began to turn them over
carefully, looking under each.

Presently Peter sneezed—'Kerty-
schoo!' Mr. McGregor was after him
in no time.

AND tried to put his foot upon Peter, who jumped out of a window, upsetting three plants. The window was too small for Mr. McGregor, and he was tired of running after Peter. He went back to his work.

PETER sat down to rest; he was out of breath and trembling with fright, and he had not the least idea which way to go. Also he was very damp with sitting in that can.

After a time he began to wander about, going lippity—lippity—not very fast, and looking all round.

HE found a door in a wall; but it was locked, and there was no room for a fat little rabbit to squeeze underneath.

An old mouse was running in and out over the stone doorstep, carrying peas and beans to her family in the wood. Peter asked her the way to the gate, but she had such a large pea in her mouth that she could not answer. She only shook her head at him. Peter began to cry.

THEN he tried to find his way straight across the garden, but he became more and more puzzled. Presently, he came to a pond where Mr. McGregor filled his water-cans. A white cat was staring at some gold-fish, she sat very, very still, but now and then the tip of her tail twitched as if it were alive. Peter thought it best to go away without speaking to her; he had heard about cats from his cousin, little Benjamin Bunny.

H^E went back towards the tool-shed, but suddenly, quite close to him, he heard the noise of a hoe—scr-r-ritch, scratch, scratch, scritch. Peter scuttered underneath the bushes. But presently, as nothing happened, he came out, and climbed upon a wheel-barrow and peeped over. The first thing he saw was Mr. McGregor hoeing onions. His back was turned towards Peter, and beyond him was the gate!

PETER got down very quietly off the wheelbarrow, and started running as fast as he could go, along a straight walk behind some black-currant bushes.

Mr. McGregor caught sight of him at the corner, but Peter did not care. He slipped underneath the gate, and was safe at last in the wood outside the garden.

MR. McGREGOR hung up the little jacket and the shoes for a scare-crow to frighten the blackbirds.

PETER never stopped running or looked behind him till he got home to the big fir-tree.

He was so tired that he flopped down upon the nice soft sand on the floor of the rabbit-hole and shut his eyes. His mother was busy cooking; she wondered what he had done with his clothes. It was the second little jacket and pair of shoes that Peter had lost in a fortnight!

I AM sorry to say that Peter was not
very well during the evening.

His mother put him to bed, and
made some camomile tea; and she gave
a dose of it to Peter!

'One table-spoonful to be taken at
bed-time.'

BUT Flopsy, Mopsy, and Cotton-tail had bread and milk and blackberries for supper.

The Tale of Tom Kitten

ONCE upon a time there were three little kittens, and their names were Mittens, Tom Kitten, and Moppet.

They had dear little fur coats of their own; and they tumbled about the doorstep and played in the dust.

BUT one day their mother—Mrs. Tabitha Twitchit—expected friends to tea; so she fetched the kittens indoors, to wash and dress them, before the fine company arrived.

FIRST she scrubbed their faces (this one is Moppet).

THEN she brushed their fur (this
one is Mittens).

THEN she combed their tails and whiskers (this is Tom Kitten).

Tom was very naughty, and he scratched.

MRS. TABITHA dressed Moppet
and Mittens in clean pinafores
and tuckers; and then she took all
sorts of elegant uncomfortable clothes
out of a chest of drawers, in order to
dress up her son Thomas.

TOM KITTEN was very fat, and
he had grown; several buttons
burst off. His mother sewed them on
again.

WHEN the three kittens were ready, Mrs. Tabitha unwisely turned them out into the garden, to be out of the way while she made hot buttered toast.

'Now keep your frocks clean, children! You must walk on your hind legs. Keep away from the dirty ash-pit, and from Sally Henny Penny, and from the pig-stye and the Puddle-Ducks.'

MOPPET and Mittens walked down the garden path unsteadily. Presently they trod upon their pinafores and fell on their noses.

When they stood up there were several green smears!

'LET us climb up the rockery, and sit on the garden wall,' said Moppet.

They turned their pinafores back to front, and went up with a skip and a jump; Moppet's white tucker fell down into the road.

TOM KITTEN was quite unable to jump when walking upon his hind legs in trousers. He came up the rockery by degrees, breaking the ferns, and shedding buttons right and left.

H E was all in pieces when he reached the top of the wall.

Moppet and Mittens tried to pull him together; his hat fell off, and the rest of his buttons burst.

WHILE they were in difficulties, there was a pit pat paddle pat! and the three Puddle-Ducks came along the hard high road, marching one behind the other and doing the goose step—pit pat paddle pat! pit pat waddle pat!

THEY stopped and stood in a row,
and stared up at the kittens. They
had very small eyes and looked sur-
prised.

THEN the two duck-birds, Rebeccah
and Jemima Puddle-Duck, picked
up the hat and tucker and put them
on.

MITTENS laughed so that she fell off the wall. Moppet and Tom descended after her; the pinafores and all the rest of Tom's clothes came off on the way down.

'Come! Mr. Drake Puddle-Duck,' said Moppet—'Come and help us to dress him! Come and button up Tom!'

MR. DRAKE PUDDLE-DUCK
advanced in a slow sideways man-
ner, and picked up the various articles.

BUT he put them on *himself!* They fitted him even worse than Tom Kitten.

'It's a very fine morning!' said Mr. Drake Puddle-Duck.

AND he and Jemima and Rebeccah Puddle-Duck set off up the road, keeping step—pit pat, paddle pat! pit pat, waddle pat!

THEN Tabitha Twitchit came down the garden and found her kittens on the wall with no clothes on.

SHE pulled them off the wall, smacked them, and took them back to the house.

'My friends will arrive in a minute, and you are not fit to be seen; I am affronted,' said Mrs. Tabitha Twitchit.

SHE sent them upstairs; and I am sorry to say she told her friends that they were in bed with the measles; which was not true.

QUITE the contrary; they were not
in bed: *not* in the least.

Somehow there were very extraordi-
nary noises over-head, which disturbed
the dignity and repose of the tea party.

A ND I think that some day I shall
have to make another, larger, book,
to tell you more about Tom Kitten!

AS for the Puddle-Ducks—they went into a pond.

The clothes all came off directly, because there were no buttons.

AND Mr. Drake Puddle-Duck, and Jemima and Rebeccah, have been looking for them ever since.

The Tale of Squirrel Nutkin

THIS is a Tale about a tail—a tail
that belonged to a little red squirrel,
and his name was Nutkin.

He had a brother called Twinkleberry, and a great many cousins: they
lived in a wood at the edge of a lake.

IN the middle of the lake there is an island covered with trees and nut bushes; and amongst those trees stands a hollow oak-tree, which is the house of an owl who is called Old Brown.

ONE autumn when the nuts were ripe, and the leaves on the hazel bushes were golden and green—Nutkin and Twinkleberry and all the other little squirrels came out of the wood, and down to the edge of the lake.

THEY made little rafts out of twigs,
and they paddled away over the
water to Owl Island to gather nuts.

Each squirrel had a little sack and a
large oar, and spread out his tail for a
sail.

THEY also took with them an offer-
ing of three fat mice as a present
for Old Brown, and put them down
upon his door-step.

Then Twinkleberry and the other
little squirrels each made a low bow,
and said politely—

'Old Mr. Brown, will you favour us
with permission to gather nuts upon
your island?'

BUT Nutkin was excessively impertinent in his manners. He bobbed up and down like a little red *cherry*, singing—

'Riddle me, riddle me, rot-tot-tote!
A little wee man, in a red red coat!
A staff in his hand, and a stone in his throat;
If you'll tell me this riddle, I'll give you a groat.'

Now this riddle is as old as the hills; Mr. Brown paid no attention whatever to Nutkin.

He shut his eyes obstinately and went to sleep.

THE squirrels filled their little sacks
with nuts, and sailed away home
in the evening.

BUT next morning they all came
back again to Owl Island; and
Twinkleberry and the others brought
a fine fat mole, and laid it on the
stone in front of Old Brown's doorway,
and said—

'Mr. Brown, will you favour us with
your gracious permission to gather
some more nuts?'

B^{UT} Nutkin, who had no respect,
began to dance up and down, tick-
ling old Mr. Brown with a *nettle* and
singing—

> 'Old Mr. B! Riddle-me-ree!
> Hitty Pitty within the wall,
> Hitty Pitty without the wall;
> If you touch Hitty Pitty,
> Hitty Pitty will bite you!'

Mr. Brown woke up suddenly and
carried the mole into his house.

HE shut the door in Nutkin's face.
Presently a little thread of blue
smoke from a wood fire came up from
the top of the tree, and Nutkin peeped
through the key-hole and sang—

    ' A house full, a hole full!
    And you cannot gather a bowl-full!'

THE squirrels searched for nuts all over the island and filled their little sacks.

But Nutkin gathered oak-apples— yellow and scarlet—and sat upon a beech-stump playing marbles, and watching the door of old Mr. Brown.

ON the third day the squirrels got
up very early and went fishing;
they caught seven fat minnows as a
present for Old Brown.

They paddled over the lake and
landed under a crooked chestnut tree
on Owl Island.

TWINKLEBERRY and six other little squirrels each carried a fat minnow; but Nutkin, who had no nice manners, brought no present at all. He ran in front, singing—

'The man in the wilderness said to me,
"How many strawberries grow in the sea?"
I answered him as I thought good—
"As many red herrings as grow in the wood."'

But old Mr. Brown took no interest in riddles—not even when the answer was provided for him.

ON the fourth day the squirrels brought a present of six fat beetles, which were as good as plums in *plum-pudding* for Old Brown. Each beetle was wrapped up carefully in a dock-leaf, fastened with a pine-needle pin.

But Nutkin sang as rudely as ever—

'Old Mr. B! riddle-me-ree
  Flour of England, fruit of Spain,
  Met together in a shower of rain;
  Put in a bag tied round with a string,
If you'll tell me this riddle, I'll give you a ring!'

Which was ridiculous of Nutkin, because he had not got any ring to give to Old Brown.

THE other squirrels hunted up and down the nut bushes; but Nutkin gathered robin's pin-cushions off a briar bush, and stuck them full of pine-needle pins.

ON the fifth day the squirrels brought a present of wild honey; it was so sweet and sticky that they licked their fingers as they put it down upon the stone. They had stolen it out of a bumble *bees'* nest on the tippitty top of the hill.

But Nutkin skipped up and down, singing—

'Hum-a-bum! buzz! buzz! Hum-a-bum buzz!
    As I went over Tipple-tine
    I met a flock of bonny swine;
Some yellow-nacked, some yellow backed!
    They were the very bonniest swine
    That e'er went over Tipple-tine.'

ON the sixth day, which was Saturday, the squirrels came again for the last time; they brought a new-laid *egg* in a little rush basket as a last parting present for Old Brown.

But Nutkin ran in front laughing, and shouting—

'Humpty Dumpty lies in the beck,
With a white counterpane round his neck,
Forty doctors and forty wrights,
Cannot put Humpty Dumpty to rights!'

NOW old Mr. Brown took an interest in eggs; he opened one eye and shut it again. But still he did not speak.

NUTKIN became more and more impertinent—

'Old Mr. B! Old Mr. B!
Hickamore, Hackamore, on the King's kitchen door;
All the King's horses, and all the King's men,
Couldn't drive Hickamore, Hackamore,
Off the King's kitchen door.'

Nutkin danced up and down like a *sunbeam*; but still Old Brown said nothing at all.

Nutkin began again—

'Arthur O'Bower has broken his band,
He comes roaring up the land!
The King of Scots with all his power,
Cannot turn Arthur of the Bower!'

NUTKIN made a whirring noise to sound like the *wind*, and he took a running jump right onto the head of Old Brown!....

Then all at once there was a flutterment and a scufflement and a loud 'Squeak!'

The other squirrels scuttered away into the bushes.

WHEN they came back very cautiously, peeping round the tree—there was Old Brown sitting on his door-step, quite still, with his eyes closed, as if nothing had happened.

*   *   *   *   *

But Nutkin was in his waist-coat pocket!

THIS looks like the end of the story; but it isn't.

OLD BROWN carried Nutkin into
his house, and held him up by the
tail, intending to skin him; but Nutkin
pulled so very hard that his tail broke
in two, and he dashed up the staircase
and escaped out of the attic window.

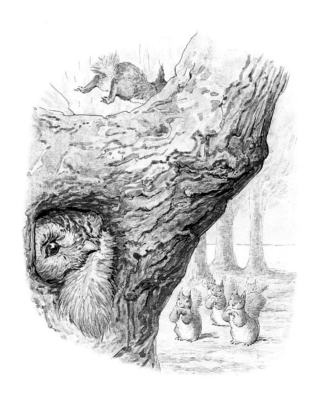

AND to this day, if you meet Nutkin
up a tree and ask him a riddle, he
will throw sticks at you, and stamp his
feet and scold, and shout—
  'Cuck-cuck-cuck-cur-r-r-cuck-k-k!'

The Tale of Johnny Town-Mouse

JOHNNY TOWN-MOUSE was born in a cupboard. Timmy Willie was born in a garden. Timmy Willie was a little country mouse who went to town by mistake in a hamper. The gardener sent vegetables to town once a week by carrier; he packed them in a big hamper.

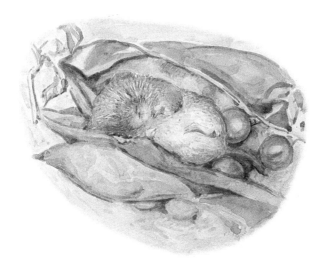

THE gardener left the hamper by
the garden gate, so that the carrier
could pick it up when he passed.
Timmy Willie crept in through a hole
in the wicker-work, and after eating
some peas—Timmy Willie fell fast
asleep.

HE awoke in a fright, while the hamper was being lifted into the carrier's cart. Then there was a jolting, and a clattering of horse's feet; other packages were thrown in; for miles and miles—jolt—jolt—jolt! and Timmy Willie trembled amongst the jumbled up vegetables.

AT last the cart stopped at a house,
where the hamper was taken out,
carried in, and set down. The cook
gave the carrier sixpence; the back
door banged, and the cart rumbled
away. But there was no quiet; there
seemed to be hundreds of carts passing.
Dogs barked; boys whistled in the
street; the cook laughed, the parlour
maid ran up and down-stairs; and a
canary sang like a steam engine.

TIMMY WILLIE, who had lived all his life in a garden, was almost frightened to death. Presently the cook opened the hamper and began to unpack the vegetables. Out sprang the terrified Timmy Willie.

UP jumped the cook on a chair, exclaiming 'A mouse! a mouse! Call the cat! Fetch me the poker, Sarah!' Timmy Willie did not wait for Sarah with the poker; he rushed along the skirting board till he came to a little hole, and in he popped.

THE dinner was of eight courses; not much of anything, but truly elegant. All the dishes were unknown to Timmy Willie, who would have been a little afraid of tasting them; only he was very hungry, and very anxious to behave with company manners. The continual noise upstairs made him so nervous, that he dropped a plate. 'Never mind, they don't belong to us,' said Johnny.

'WHY don't those youngsters come back with the dessert?' It should be explained that two young mice, who were waiting on the others, went skirmishing upstairs to the kitchen between courses. Several times they had come tumbling in, squeaking and laughing; Timmy Willie learnt with horror that they were being chased by the cat. His appetite failed, he felt faint. 'Try some jelly?' said Johnny Town-mouse.

'NO? Would you rather go to bed? I will show you a most comfortable sofa pillow.'

The sofa pillow had a hole in it. Johnny Town-mouse quite honestly recommended it as the best bed, kept exclusively for visitors. But the sofa smelt of cat. Timmy Willie preferred to spend a miserable night under the fender.

IT was just the same next day. An
excellent breakfast was provided—for
mice accustomed to eat bacon; but
Timmy Willie had been reared on
roots and salad. Johnny Town-mouse
and his friends racketted about under
the floors, and came boldly out all over
the house in the evening. One partic-
ularly loud crash had been caused by
Sarah tumbling downstairs with the
tea-tray; there were crumbs and sugar
and smears of jam to be collected, in
spite of the cat.

TIMMY WILLIE longed to be at
home in his peaceful nest in a
sunny bank. The food disagreed with
him; the noise prevented him from
sleeping. In a few days he grew so
thin that Johnny Town-mouse noticed
it, and questioned him. He listened to
Timmy Willie's story and inquired
about the garden. ' It sounds rather a
dull place? What do you do when it
rains? '

'WHEN it rains, I sit in my little sandy burrow and shell corn and seeds from my Autumn store. I peep out at the throstles and blackbirds on the lawn, and my friend Cock Robin. And when the sun comes out again, you should see my garden and the flowers—roses and pinks and pansies— no noise except the birds and bees, and the lambs in the meadows.'

THE winter passed; the sun came out again; Timmy Willie sat by his burrow warming his little fur coat and sniffing the smell of violets and spring grass. He had nearly forgotten his visit to town. When up the sandy path all spick and span with a brown leather bag came Johnny Town-mouse!

TIMMY WILLIE received him with open arms. 'You have come at the best of all the year, we will have herb pudding and sit in the sun.'

'H'm'm! it is a little damp,' said Johnny Town-mouse, who was carrying his tail under his arm, out of the mud.

'WHAT is that fearful noise?' he started violently.

'That?' said Timmy Willie, 'that is only a cow; I will beg a little milk, they are quite harmless, unless they happen to lie down upon you. How are all our friends?'

JOHNNY'S account was rather mid-
dling. He explained why he was
paying his visit so early in the season;
the family had gone to the seaside for
Easter; the cook was doing spring
cleaning, on board wages, with particular instructions to clear out the mice.
There were four kittens, and the cat
had killed the canary.

'THEY say we did it; but I know
better,' said Johnny Town-mouse.
'Whatever is that fearful racket?'

'That is only the lawnmower; I will
fetch some of the grass clippings presently to make your bed. I am sure you
had better settle in the country,
Johnny.'

'H'M 'M—we shall see by Tuesday week; the hamper is stopped while they are at the sea-side.'

'I am sure you will never want to live in town again,' said Timmy Willie.